To you, Mom and Dad, our supportive family. And to the Chichis and Didis everywhere, who are learning to love and embrace who they are.
—PA + NA

To Ben. Thanks for giving me your last name. And to the bird that made it all possible. —HB

Chichi and Didi Love Their Names

written by
Peace Amadi and Ndidi Amadi

illustrated by
Hayley Blackwood

"I'm so excited for the first day of school today!" Chichi says.

"Me too!" Didi replies.

"I heard Ms. Jackson brings her pet turtle to class," Chichi says. "I hope we get to feed it."

"Oh cool!" Didi says. "I hope Mr. Lopez has a cheetah."

"A cheetah?" The sisters burst into giggles.

Knock, knock.

"Hello, my queens," Mama says. "Are you ready to go?"

After Mama drops them off, Chichi walks Didi to her kindergarten class.

There's no cheetah in sight, but Didi is happy with the fuzzy rug and all the bright colors.

Ms. Jackson is at the door of Chichi's second-grade classroom, greeting each student with a smile and a high five.

As Chichi looks around for who might be a new friend, she spots the class turtle on Ms. Jackson's desk.

This is going to be a good year, Chichi thinks.

Riiiinng!

Ms. Jackson begins to take roll.

"Lawrence?"

"Here!" a boy with freckles loudly replies.

"Brittany?"

"Here!"

Chichi thinks Brittany's braids and hot-pink sneakers are cool.

"Corey?"

"Here!"

Chichi likes his tight curly hair.

Chichi waits for Ms. Jackson to call the next name, but instead there is a long pause.

"Chuh . . . Chuh . . ." Ms. Jackson begins. "Oh my! This is a different name. It's spelled C-h-i-n-y-e-r-e."

"That's me!" Chichi says. "But you can call me Chichi."

Chichi wishes she could pull her head into a shell like the class turtle.

At dinner, Chichi picks at her jollof rice.

"It's time for everyone to share about their day," Daddy says. "Who would like to go first?"

"Me!" Didi says.

"I made a lot of friends at recess, and I had chicken nuggets for lunch." She goes on and on about the favorite parts of her first day of kindergarten.

"That sounds like a good day," Mama says.

Daddy looks at Chichi next.

But Chichi stays silent.

"What about you, Chichi?" Daddy asks caringly.

Chichi tries not to cry, but her eyes fill with tears.

"When my teacher took roll, she couldn't say my name. When I told her my name was Chichi, the whole class laughed at me!"

"Oh, Chichi, that must've hurt your feelings," Mama says.

Daddy strokes his chin. This is the sign that Daddy has a lesson to share.

"Chichi, did you know that names are very important?" he asks. "In our culture, we believe names **tell a story** about who you are and who you will become. Names carry **hope** and **purpose** for the future."

"Your name means **God's gift**," he continues.
"You are a gift to us, and your Mama and I believe you will be a gift to the world."

"What about me?" Didi asks. "Does my name mean something?"

Mama laughs. "Of course, my daughter. Your name, Ndidi, means **patience**. We gave you that name as a reminder that no matter what, good things are on the way."

"Wow! IN-dee-dee!" Didi says. **"I love my name."**

"Very good!" Daddy says. "I want you and your sister to say your names with pride."

"Beautiful Chichi, hold your head high," Mama adds. "You can show your pride tomorrow."

The next day, Chichi walks into her class and spots Lawrence. Her stomach churns. She doesn't want to be laughed at again.

Ms. Jackson begins taking roll.

Once again, Ms. Jackson pauses.

But this time, Chichi remembers what her parents told her: *Names are very important. You are God's gift. Hold your head high.*

Chichi raises her hand.

"I was just about to call on you," Ms. Jackson says. "Would you like to say your name again?"

Chichi nods her head and takes a big, deep breath. All of a sudden, she feels strong. She feels proud.

"My name is Chinyere.

CHEEN -Yeh -Reh.

In my Nigerian language, my name means 'God's gift.' But you can call me Chichi."

"**What a beautiful name!**" Ms. Jackson says. "Thank you for sharing that with us, Chichi."

"Yeah, that's a cool name," Corey says.

"Hmm . . . I'm going to ask my mom what my name means!" Lawrence says.

After school, Chichi picks up Didi from her classroom.

"Did they laugh at your name today?" Didi asks.

"No. I did what Mama and Daddy told us to," Chichi says. "I said my name with pride."

"Good. Me too. **I love my name!**" Didi says.

"I love my name too!"
Chichi beams with pride.

Text copyright © 2025 by Chinyere Peace Amadi and Ndidi Amadi
Cover art and interior illustrations copyright © 2025 by Hayley Blackwood

Penguin Random House values and supports copyright. Copyright fuels creativity, encourages diverse voices, promotes free speech, and creates a vibrant culture. Thank you for buying an authorized edition of this book and for complying with copyright laws by not reproducing, scanning, or distributing any part of it in any form without permission. You are supporting writers and allowing Penguin Random House to continue to publish books for every reader. Please note that no part of this book may be used or reproduced in any manner for the purpose of training artificial intelligence technologies or systems.

All rights reserved. Published in the United States by WaterBrook, an imprint of Random House, a division of Penguin Random House LLC.

WATERBROOK and colophon are registered trademarks of Penguin Random House LLC.

Originally self-published by the authors in 2019.

Hardback ISBN 978-0-593-58003-5
Ebook ISBN 978-0-593-58004-2

The Library of Congress catalog record is available at https://lccn.loc.gov/2022040091.

Printed in China

waterbrookmultnomah.com

9 8 7 6 5 4 3 2 1

First Edition

Book and cover design by Lisa Schneller Bieser